I Am Queen Ruby!

By Voncille Y. Chaney

ISBN: 099928360X
ISBN-13: 978-0999283608

For Ahmai R. Chaney-Smith,
I love you with all of my heart!

For Carl Chaney, Emily C. Chaney, Shantel C. Chaney, and Francesca C. Chaney.
Thank you for you continued support.

For Every Brown Girl-
I hope this inspires you to discover the Queen inside of you!

Ruby is a new student who has darker skin

than all of the other children at school.

Even her mother, father, and baby brother

Henry are lighter shades of brown.

On open school night, Ruby is very excited to show off her artwork. As she picks up her favorite drawing, another student named Jessica walks by with her mom. She turns around when she hears Ruby shout, "Mommy, Daddy, look at this!"

The next day after lunch, Ruby runs up to the other students as they are about to play. "No, she's not playing with us because she's adopted," Jessica yells. "I'm not adopted," Ruby replies. "Why don't you look like your family then?" asks Jessica.

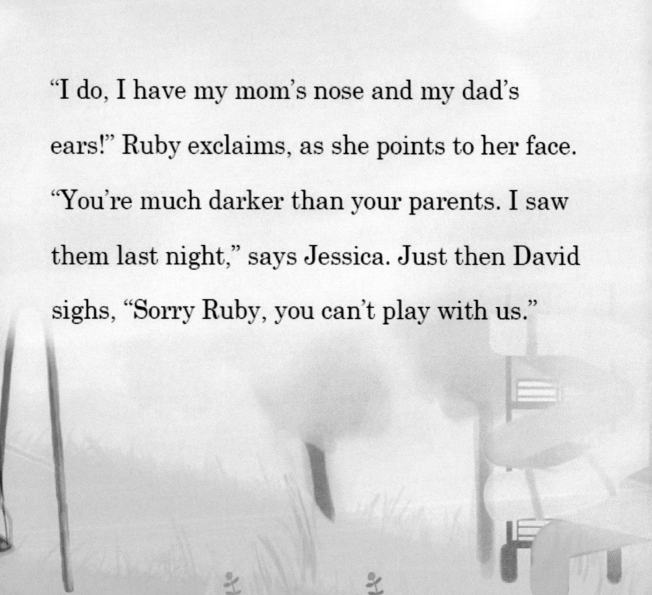

"I do, I have my mom's nose and my dad's ears!" Ruby exclaims, as she points to her face. "You're much darker than your parents. I saw them last night," says Jessica. Just then David sighs, "Sorry Ruby, you can't play with us."

For the next few weeks recess becomes

the saddest time of day for Ruby. She

watches the other students have fun, as

she sits alone at the water fountain.

One day on Ruby's way to the restroom, she hears noises coming from the auditorium. She pushes the door open and pokes her head in. Ruby sees the fourth graders rehearsing for their play with Ms. Diego, the Theater teacher.

She goes back the next day, and the next day, staying a little longer each time. One day she hears a voice behind her ask, "Would you like to be up there one day?" Before thinking, she responds with excitement, "I sure would! Oh, I didn't realize it was you, Ms. Diego."

"That's ok Ruby, I can tell you really like this play. I just wrote a new one, and I have a role that would be perfect for you," Ms. Diego says. "What role is it?" asks Ruby. "The Queen. Would you like to be the Queen in the new school play?" Ms. Diego responds. "I would love to!" Ruby says cheerfully.

After rehearsing for a few weeks, it is time for the play. Ms. Diego pulls Ruby aside and tells her that when she was a little girl, she was teased about having different hair. "Really?" Ruby sighs. "Yes, so I began writing plays to show people that we are all different in our own unique way", says Ms. Diego.

Ms. Diego then takes Ruby to the mirror and asks her, "What do you see?" At first Ruby shrugs her shoulders, as she replies, "A dark brown girl." Ms. Diego whispers, "Do you want to know what I see?" Ruby says, "Yes," as she nods her head.

"Well…" Ms. Diego says, "I see a Queen, but not just any Queen. I see Queen Ruby!" After looking into the mirror, Ruby replies, "Oh yeah, I see her too". Ms. Diego asks her again, "Who do you see?" Ruby exclaims, "Queen Ruby." Then Ms. Diego asks, "And who are you?"

Ruby shouts, "I am Queen Ruby!"

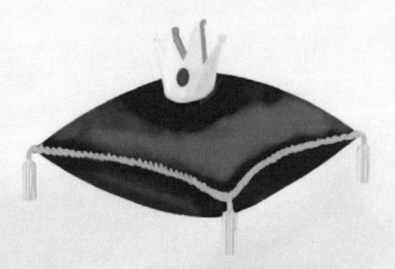

Made in the USA
Middletown, DE
26 May 2022